froglets
Fairy Tales

The Little Red Hen

D1136253

Franklin Watts
First published in Great Britain in 2006 by
The Watts Publishing Group

Text © Penny Dolan 2006
Illustration © Beccy Blake 2006

www.fsc.org

MIX

**Paper from
responsible sources**

FSC® C104740

A CIP catalogue record for this book is available
from the British Library.

ISBN 978 0 7496 6585 2 (pbk)

Series Editor: Jackie Hamley
Series Advisor: Dr Barrie Wade
Series Designer: Peter Scoulding

Printed in China

Franklin Watts
An imprint of
Hachette Children's Group
Part of The Watts Publishing Group
Carmelite House
50 Victoria Embankment
London EC4Y 0DZ

An Hachette UK Company
www.hachette.co.uk

www.franklinwatts.co.uk

The Little Red Hen

Retold by Penny Dolan

Illustrated by Beccy Blake

W
FRANKLIN WATTS
LONDON•SYDNEY

Little Red Hen found
some grains of wheat.

"Who will help me plant them?" asked Little Red Hen.

"Not I!"
said Cat.

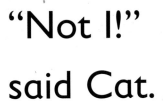

"Not I!"
said Dog.

"Not I!"
said Rat.

"Then I must do it myself," she said.

8

The Ratty
Times

9

The wheat grew, but
the weeds grew, too.
"Who will help me weed?"
asked Little Red Hen.

"Not I!" said Cat.
"Not I!" said Dog.
"Not I!" said Rat.

"Then I must do it myself!"
she said.

The wheat grew ripe.

"Who will help me cut the wheat?" asked Little Red Hen.

14

"Not I!" yawned Cat.
"Not I!" yawned Dog.
"Not I!" yawned Rat.

"Then I must harvest it myself," she said.

"Who will help me carry the wheat?" asked Little Red Hen.

"Not I!" grumbled Cat.
"Not I!" grumbled Dog.
"Not I!" grumbled Rat.

"Then I must carry it to the mill myself," she said.

The miller ground the wheat into flour.

"Who will help me make and bake my bread?" asked Little Red Hen.

Nobody answered.
"Then I will make
and bake it myself!"

Cat, Dog and Rat smelt
something delicious.

"Who will help me eat my bread?" called Little Red Hen.

"Me!" said Cat.

"Me!" said Dog.

"Me, me, me!" said Rat.

"Who is asking you?"
laughed Little Red Hen.

"I am calling all my little chicks to help me eat my bread!"

Look out for more stories!

Froglets (formerly known as Leapfrog) has been specially designed to support children beginning to read independently. Look out for more stories!

For more Froglets books go to: www.franklinwatts.co.uk